To:

From:

# Endorsements

If kids can learn to navigate iPads at age two, they can learn the Bible. If they can repeat the dialogue of *Bubble Guppies* when they are preschoolers, they can learn the Bible. Using our bestselling volume *The Joshua Code* as inspiration, Holly Shivers challenges our children to memorize Scripture alongside their parents in this beautifully illustrated book. It is not about getting our kids into the Word; it is about getting the Word into our kids. Our hope is that they will hide the Word in their young hearts so they might not sin against God. Holly engages and connects, speaking the language children understand so they can confidently confess, "I can learn the Bible!"

—O. S. Hawkins, author of *The Joshua Code: 52 Scripture Verses Every Believer Should Know* and *The Jesus Code: 52 Scripture Questions Every Believer Should Answer*

As parents and as believers in Jesus Christ, we know we are called to teach our kids about Jesus and His Word. However, unpacking complex scriptures to our two young boys isn't easy. *I Can Learn the Bible* equips us to confidently interpret what can be confusing to our kids. Its creative language and effortless outline make teaching Scripture manageable and fun.

—Tony Romo, quarterback of the Dallas Cowboys, and Candice Romo, journalist

This is a delightful and important book. What greater gift can we give our children than the Word of God tucked deep into their hearts? We live in precarious times, and the only thing that will not shift and change is God's Word. I love and highly recommend this book.

—Sheila Walsh, author of *God's Little Princess Bedtime Devotional*

In a world where the deterioration of our society is so prevalent and the pressures our kids are facing are tremendous, the need for children to learn God's Word and be equipped with truth is more important than ever before. *I Can Learn the Bible* is an easy-to-use children's devotional that nurtures the ability to hide God's Word in one's heart. It provides the foundational basics that a child needs to get started.

—Linda Paulk, president and CEO of Sky Ranches, Inc.

This book is an innovative and exciting way to teach the Scriptures to children. Holly has used *every* one of these creative illustrations with her own children. How amazing that she is willing to share her personal insights with others. You will love teaching your children from this challenging book.

—Sondra Saunders, children's minister for 52 years

We can't think of anything more important for parents than helping our children to love, learn, and live God's Word. Holly Shivers provides an incredible tool to teach and train our children in this prayerful journey of faith. Parents, get this book and use it with your kids, and then celebrate what God does in their lives.

—Dr. Jack Graham, pastor of Prestonwood Baptist Church, and Deb Graham, director of ministry resources at Prestonwood Baptist Church

My friend Holly Shivers has given parents and children alike an invaluable tool. There is nothing more important than children learning from the pages of the Bible just how much God knows and loves them. And Holly has come alongside parents to help them help their children discover the mind-blowing, heartwarming message that Jesus has secured for them what they can never secure for themselves. Thank you, Holly!

—Tullian Tchividjian, pastor of Coral Ridge Presbyterian Church and author of *One Way Love: Inexhaustible Grace for an Exhausted World*

The JOSHUA CODE for Kids

# I Can Learn the Bible

## 52 Scriptures Every Kid Should Know

By Holly Hawkins Shivers

Tommy NELSON®
A Division of Thomas Nelson Publishers
NASHVILLE MEXICO CITY RIO DE JANEIRO

Published in Nashville, Tennessee, by Tommy Nelson. Tommy Nelson is an imprint of Thomas Nelson. Thomas Nelson is a registered trademark of HarperCollins Christian Publishing, Inc.

Tommy Nelson titles may be purchased in bulk for educational, business, fund-raising, or sales promotional use. For information, please e-mail SpecialMarkets@ThomasNelson.com.



**Library of Congress Cataloging-in-Publication Data**

Shivers, Holly Hawkins, author.
I can learn the Bible : the Joshua code for kids : 52 devotions and scriptures for kids / by Holly Hawkins Shivers.
pages cm
Audience: Ages 4-8.
ISBN 978-0-529-10899-9 (hardcover)
1. Devotional literature--Juvenile literature. 2. Children--Prayers and devotions. 3. Devotional calendars--Juvenile literature. 4. Christian life--Juvenile literature. I. Hawkins, O. S. Joshua code. II. Title.
BV4870.S525 2014
242.62--dc23
2014016182

*Printed in Bosnia and Heregovina*

24 25 26 GPS 10 9 8 7

Mfr: GPS Group/June 2024/PO #12274351

# Table of Contents

# Foreword

"If you give your child one thing by the age of five, let it be a big faith in God."

When I heard my seminary professor Howard Hendricks say these words, I had two children under five and one on the way. I worried how I would give these little minds and hearts in my care a big view of God. I wanted help. I needed words and pictures that could bring God's Word to life for them and unleash an expansive view of God in their imaginations and souls.

I believe the reason my professor said these words is that there's nothing more beautiful or powerful than the simplicity of childlike faith. God moves through faith.

To children's minds, God is real. God is not complicated. God is limitless. God loves them. God is God, and that is all there is to it. Oh, how we complicate Him and everything else as we mature.

Proverbs 22:6 says, "Start children off on the way they should go, and even when they are old they will not turn from it" (NIV).

Holly hasn't just written a beautiful book; she has created a tool to build big faith in little minds.

I pray that these words and stories will expand your child's view of God and His great love. And perhaps as you read, God will become even bigger to you as well.

As you read this book, remember that our God is real. Our God is limitless. Our God loves you. Our God has not forgotten you. Our God is God, and that is all there is to it.

May your faith run wild, and may you draw near to Jesus in these words.

Jennie Allen
Mother of four
Author of *Restless*
Founder of IF: Gathering

# Letter to Parents

A common struggle exists among Christian parents today: as our culture moves further and further from the truths of God's Word, how can we influence our children to love God and follow His purposes for their lives? I believe Joshua 1:8 gives us an answer: "This Book of the Law shall not depart from your mouth, but you shall meditate in it day and night, that you may observe to do according to all that is written in it. For then you will make your way prosperous, and then you will have good success" (NKJV).

You see, we can educate our children with a biblical worldview, we can enroll them in church activities and teach them principles to the best of our abilities, and we can pray for them, discipline them, and love them well. But there is nothing like the Word of God being planted in their hearts, taking root, and producing genuine spiritual growth. Ultimately, the spiritual well-being of our children rests in the hands of God—He will form and strengthen them through His Word and His Spirit. It takes the pressure off parents, does it not? That is why I love Joshua 1:8. And perhaps this verse is best applied to these little ones who are just starting this life journey. We cannot make every "right" decision for our children, nor should we. We cannot be ever present, and the older they become, the less and less they need us. That is why we must do what we can while they are young. We want to turn them toward the one thing—rather, the one Person—who *will* be there for them: the Person of Jesus Christ and His living, active Word hidden deep in their hearts.

This book is designed for parents and children to read together. Questions and fill-in-the-blank statements throughout the text will help prompt discussion. Each week's devotion has a key verse to meditate on and commit to memory. Your weekly schedule may look something like this:

Monday: Read the devotional and have your child read or repeat the Bible verse.

Tuesday: Have your child memorize the first phrase of the verse. Talk about what it means and ask questions.

Wednesday: Memorize the middle part of the verse. Talk and ask questions while you work on saying the first and middle part of the verse.

Thursday: Memorize the last part of the verse.

Talk and ask questions while you work on saying the entire verse.

Friday: Reread the devotional and recite the entire verse.

Saturday and Sunday: Continue to review and recite the scripture until it is sealed forever in that little heart and mind!

In these devotionals your child will hear one particular truth over and over again until she can say it backward: "God's Word is *for me* and *to me*, it is *in me* and working *through me*, and just like His love, it goes on and on forever!" May the Lord Himself go before you on this journey as you give your child something so valuable . . . that no one can ever take away.

**In the beginning God created the sky and the earth.**

**Genesis 1:1**

## Week 1

# Your View of the World

Have you ever tried on a pair of glasses that did not belong to you? Things look very different, don't they? Like looking through different glasses, every person looks at the world in a certain way. We call this a *worldview*. The way we see our world affects how we live and the choices we make. So what you believe is very important. Some people think the world happened for no reason—it just appeared out of nowhere in one big *poof!* Others are not sure how it came to be, and don't really know why they are here. The very first verse in the Bible gives us the correct glasses that fit perfectly, and through which everything looks crystal clear. Let's answer three important questions about this verse.

## When?

"In the *beginning* . . ." This takes us back to the very beginning—before anything was, the beginning of time! Close your eyes and be as quiet as you can for ten seconds. That's what it was like in the beginning. It was dark and empty.

## Who?

Look at the next word in this verse: "In the beginning, *God* . . ." It was dark and empty, and God was there. He was in the beginning before time even began! Have you ever wondered where He came from, or how He got there? Even though it's hard to understand, the Bible tells us He was just always there. In the beginning was God.

## What?

In the beginning, what did God do? He *created* the sky and the earth. Wow! So out of darkness and emptiness, He made the whole world! What a wise, creative, amazing God we have.

**Dear Jesus, thank You for creating the world we live in. You are so great and You are so amazing. My favorite part of Your creation is . . . . . . . . . . . . .
Amen.**

Now that you understand this verse, you have a worldview! You know how we got here, and when you see a beautiful sunset, you know who painted it. As you begin memorizing your first verse this week, you are putting God's Word in your heart and mind. His Word—the Bible—is there for you, and it will never go away.

Say these words out loud:

**God's Word is *for me* and *to me*, it is *in me* and working *through me*, and just like His love, it goes on and on forever!**

"For God loved the world so much that he gave his only Son. God gave his Son so that whoever believes in him may not be lost, but have eternal life."

John 3:16

Week 2

# What Is the Gospel?

This week's verse is the most famous verse in the Bible. It is sometimes called the *gospel*, or the *good news*. God gave His only Son, Jesus, so that those of us who believe in Him could live forever with Him one day in heaven. Now *that* is good news!

## Why Did God Do This?

The first part of the verse tells us exactly why God gave His Son. "For God loved the world so much . . ." He did it because He loves us! Do you know how deep the ocean is? Do you know how wide it is from the east to the west? (It would be like starting to walk one way and never stopping!) That is how much God loves you. And do you know the best part about His love? It never ends. No matter what you do or where you go, God will never stop loving you. God loves the world *so* much.

## What Did God Do?

The second phrase in this verse tells us what God did. "He gave His only Son." That means that God has one Son, and He let Him die on a cross—for you and for me, to save us from our sins. You would have to love someone a whole lot to give up your own son, right? And Jesus, God's Son, chose to follow and obey His Father and died on a cross.

## Who Did He Do This For?

The next part of this verse says, "Whoever believes in Him may not be lost, but have eternal life." That means that if you believe in God, and if you believe

that Jesus died for you, God has promised you life forever in heaven! He did this for *you*.

God loves you so much that He gave His only Son, and if you believe in Him, you will never be lost and you will have eternal life! *And that is the gospel.*

**Dear God, thank You for loving me. Thank You for giving Your only Son for me and for Your promise of heaven. I believe in You! Amen.**

Let's say it together:

**God's Word is *for me* and *to me*, it is *in me* and working *through me*, and just like His love, it goes on and on forever!**

I mean that you have been saved by grace because you believe. You did not save yourselves. It was a gift from God. You cannot brag that you are saved by the work you have done.

Ephesians 2:8–9

Week 3

# Sin and Grace

We have learned that God loves us and sent His Son to die for us. We have also learned that if we believe in Him, He will forgive our sins and give us the promise of heaven. This week's verse is about how we can receive God's gift of grace—even though we don't deserve it.

## A Thing Called Sin

The Bible tells us that we all have sin in our lives (Romans 3:23). Have you ever told a lie? Have you ever stolen anything? Have you ever said something that was unkind? Maybe you have *not* done something, even though you knew you should have. These are all sins. When we do these things, we often feel sad inside. And because we sin and God is perfect, we can't ever be good enough to get to heaven on our own. Our sin actually *separates* us from God. Because of that sin, we deserve to be punished.

The Lord is my shepherd. I have everything I need.

Psalm 23:1

Week 4

# You Have a Shepherd

You have probably heard the story of David and Goliath. Do you know what David's job was as a young boy? He was a shepherd in the fields of Bethlehem. What do you think a shepherd is supposed to do? If you said, "Stay near his sheep, make sure they don't wander off, and protect them from wolves and other predators," then you were right! A shepherd takes good care of his sheep and protects them day and night.

## How Is the Lord Our Shepherd?

In Psalm 23, David calls God his shepherd. What do you think he means by that? He means that the Lord is always with us, He will keep us from getting lost, and He will protect us.

Do you think a shepherd walks behind or in front of his sheep? He walks in front! He leads them and shows them where they need to go. Just like a shepherd, Jesus leads the way for us.

We know that in everything God works for the good of those who love him. They are the people God called, because that was his plan.

Romans 8:28

## Week 5

# The Good and the Bad, Together

Have you ever eaten a fluffy, warm biscuit, fresh from the oven? Yum! A lot of ingredients were put into that biscuit to make it taste so good. But if you were to take a bite of the flour, just by itself, it would taste awful. Or if you licked only the baking soda off of the spoon, you might gag! Once you add all of the ingredients together, though, you get a wonderful result—a warm, delicious biscuit.

## When Bad Things Happen

Like those yucky ingredients, some things in life "taste" bad to us or make us very sad. Maybe we get hurt, or we lose someone or something we love. This week's verse teaches us that even though these things may make us sad, God can use them, along with other things in our lives, to make something good. God may choose to teach you a lesson through your sadness, or He may use you one day to help someone else who is feeling sad, just like you did. Either way, God promises us that even when bad things happen, He can actually turn them into good things and use them for a reason in our lives.

## A Wonderful Promise

Did you notice the first two words of this verse? It says, "We know." We, as children of God, can *know* that God will work everything in our lives for good. And does it say *some* things? No, it says *everything*! The last part of the verse shows us that this promise is only for those of us who love God and are part of His family.

Romans 8:28 can bring you a lot of comfort now and throughout the rest of your life. What are some

bad things that have happened to you? Can you think of a way God has used some of those things for good?

**Dear Lord, thank You for working out everything in my life for good. I love You and I believe that You only want the best for me. Please help me when I am feeling sad about . . . . . . . . . . . . . . . . . . . Help me remember that You can make bad things into good things, even when I don't understand. In Jesus' name, amen.**

This time, start with a whisper, then get louder and louder until your neighbors can hear you!

**God's Word is *for me* and *to me*, it is *in me* and working *through me*, and just like His love, it goes on and on forever!**

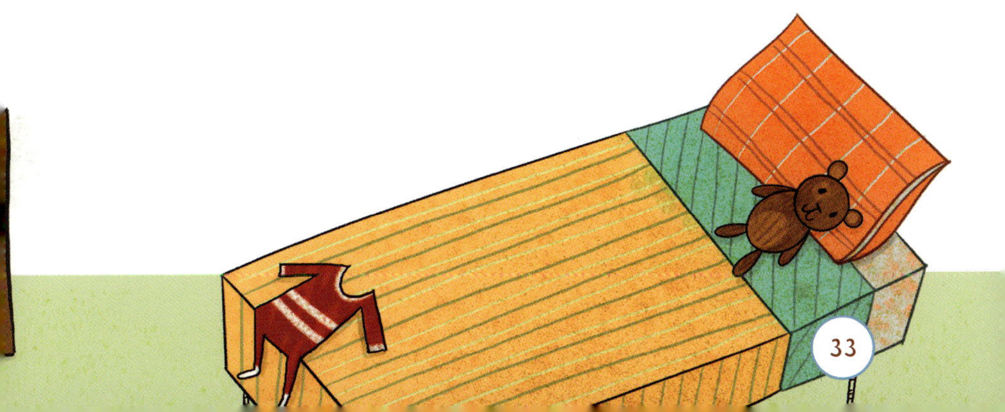

“Those who want to do right more than anything else are happy. God will fully satisfy them.”

Matthew 5:6

Week 6

# Thirsty for Doing Right

One day Jesus was teaching on a mountainside. He told all of the people listening that even if you do the right thing on the outside, it doesn't please God unless you also have the right attitude on the inside. This part of His lesson is called "The Beatitudes." Jesus teaches that we need to be who He wants us to be before we do what we think we are supposed to do. For example, if your teacher tells you to finish your math worksheet and you finish it while stomping your feet, saying unkind words, and having a bad attitude inside your heart, is Jesus pleased? No! It's not just the math worksheet He cares about—it's the attitude of your heart.

## What Is Righteousness?

When our hearts have a good attitude, we will want to do the right thing; that's called *righteousness*. It's a big word that means doing the right thing because we want to honor God, follow His laws, and live a life that pleases Him. This week's verse

We all have wandered
away like sheep.
Each of us has gone his
own way. But the Lord
has put on him the
punishment
for all the
evil we
have done.

Isaiah 53:6

Week 7

# Lost Sheep

Do you remember Psalm 23:1? Recite it! Just like that verse, our verse for this week compares us to sheep. You should know a few things about sheep:

1. **Sheep are not that smart.**
   What animals do you see doing tricks at the circus? Elephants? Monkeys? Lions? Do you ever see sheep? Not usually, because most sheep are not smart enough to learn tricks. Well, like sheep, sometimes we don't act very smart either. We choose to go our own way instead of choosing to follow God's plan for us. Have you ever gotten into trouble and thought to yourself, *Why did I do that?* You did that because you made a not-so-smart choice and went your own way instead of God's way.

2. **Sheep do not know where they are going.**
   Sheep often get lost because they have no idea where to go unless they follow the shepherd. Once they get lost, they end up

wandering around. We are like this too. If we are not following God, we will be totally lost. Can you think of some ways you can be sure to follow God's direction for you?

3. **Sheep have no way to protect themselves.** Many animals have ways to defend themselves from enemies; think about dogs, cats, porcupines, bees, and skunks. But what about sheep? They don't have any way to protect themselves—no sharp teeth or claws, no quills or stingers, not even a stinky smell! We can't protect ourselves from our enemy either. We need Jesus, our Shepherd, to protect us.

Just like sheep, we sometimes do not make smart choices, we don't know where we are going, and we have no way to defend ourselves. But "the

Lord has put on him the punishment for all of the evil we have done." This means that Jesus took our punishment and died for us, and now He is guiding and protecting us.

**Dear Jesus, I know sometimes I do not make good choices, and I choose to go my way instead of Your way. Please forgive me. Thank You for taking my sin so that I can have You as my Shepherd forever. Amen.**

Let God's Word work through you this week!

**God's Word is *for me* and *to me*, it is *in me* and working *through me*, and just like His love, it goes on and on forever!**

"Continue to ask, and God will give to you. Continue to search, and you will find. Continue to knock, and the door will open for you."

Matthew 7:7

Week 8

# Knock, Knock!

Because you are hiding God's Word in your heart every week and learning these verses, you know that God speaks to you through the Bible. But how do you speak to Him? That's right—you pray! Think about it for a second. You . . . *you* can talk to the God of the universe. You can talk to the Maker of heaven and earth, the One who made you, the Great I Am. Wow! That is a very cool thought!

## When We Ask

Our verse this week tells us how to pray and how to keep praying until we hear from God. It compares prayer to knocking on God's door—and He always answers. God wants you to talk to Him. He wants you to tell Him how you are feeling and to ask Him for help! When you ask God for things and He gives them to you, you will always remember that He heard your prayer and answered you.

## When He Answers

Do you think this verse is saying that you will get anything you ask for? Well, not exactly. God wants us to pray with His plan for us in mind. That means He wants us to ask for the things He wants for us. When you were a little two-year-old, if you asked your parents for a knife from the kitchen, do you think they would give it to you? Of course not! That would not have been what was best for you. It could have actually harmed you. Just like that, sometimes we ask for things that are not God's best for us, and when that is the case, He won't give them to us. However, if we ask for something that is part of His plan for us, we will always receive it!

Sometimes we have to ask God for something for a very long time before He gives it to us. He does not always answer us right away, but He does always answer. Do you know someone who is sick?

Do you know someone who needs to know Jesus? God wants you to keep asking, keep seeking, and keep knocking on His door as long as it takes for Him to answer.

Talk about something you want to ask God for, and then pray about it.

**Dear God, I want to ask You to . . . . . . . . . . . . . . . . . . Please hear my prayer and answer me. I love You and trust You to do what is best for me. In Jesus' name, amen.**

You are doing great! Let's hear it:

**God's Word is *for me* and *to me*, it is *in me* and working *through me*, and just like His love, it goes on and on forever!**

**Be filled with the Spirit.**

**Ephesians 5:18**

## Week 9

# Fill Me Up!

What kinds of things can you "fill up"? Let's think about it. You can fill up your cup with milk, you can fill up your car with gas, and you can fill up your stomach with your favorite ice cream! Think of a few other things you can fill up.

In our verse for this week, God is telling us to *fill ourselves up* with His Holy Spirit. Before we talk about how to do that, who is the Holy Spirit? The Holy Spirit is the One Jesus promised to send us when He went up in the clouds after He rose from the dead. The Holy Spirit is also called "the Comforter" or "the Helper." The Holy Spirit is who comes to live inside your heart when you accept Him into your life. He is always with you and He speaks to you. Is the Holy Spirit actually God? Yes, He is!

So how can we be filled with the Spirit? Ephesians 5:18–21 tells us three ways.

1. **Sing a song of praise to God.**
   What is your favorite song of worship? When you sing that song, do you think about the words and what they mean to you? God says that the first way to fill yourself up with

Him is to worship Him in song. When you are singing a song of praise to God, you are thinking about Him and you are focused on how great He is. This makes His Spirit happy and fills you up!

**2. Give thanks.**

Another way to be filled is to give thanks to God. Think about all the things He has done for you. Think about all the things He has given you. Thank Him for loving you, for choosing you to be His child, and for dying for you. Thank Him for your family, your friends, and all that you have.

**3. Put others in front of yourself.**

This passage tells us that if we want to be filled with the Spirit, we need to submit ourselves to one another. This means that you need to think about other people and

do things for them, not just think of what you want for yourself all the time.

Sing a song of praise tonight with your family. Then make a list of all of the things for which you are thankful.

**Dear Father, I want to be filled with Your Spirit! Please hear my song of praise and my prayers to You, and fill me up. Thank You, Jesus. Amen.**

This week, as you learn this verse, can you do those three things? Can you let this truth work through you? After all . . .

**God's Word is *for me* and *to me,* it is *in me* and working *through me,* and just like His love, it goes on and on forever!**

**The Spirit gives love, joy, peace, patience, kindness, goodness, faithfulness, gentleness, self-control.**

Galatians 5:22–23

Week 10

# The Fruit of the Spirit

Imagine yourself sitting high up in an apple tree. You look around, and there are apples everywhere. Do you know where those apples came from? Although the branches are what hold the fruit on the tree, the fruit actually grows because it's attached to the trunk that runs down into the ground, giving it the water and nourishment it needs. It's the same way with Jesus. He says we are just like those branches—we can't grow any fruit unless we are connected to Him. If you stay connected to Jesus through prayer and through His Word, you can grow fruit! Here is the kind of fruit we are talking about:

- **Love**—When you show this fruit, you are putting other people's needs in front of your own, and you are caring about others.
- **Joy**—This fruit is shown when you are happy and content way down inside of you . . . no matter what!
- **Peace**—This is that feeling you get when you know in your heart everything is going to be okay. It makes you feel safe and calm. Peace also can mean not fighting or arguing and getting along with everyone.

- **Patience**—This kind of fruit helps you wait and not get so angry.
- **Kindness**—This fruit is shown when you think about others before yourself and when you do something thoughtful for someone.
- **Goodness**—Goodness means living in a way that pleases God, or makes Him happy.
- **Faithfulness**—This fruit helps you never give up! It means always being there, no matter what, and doing what you say you are going to do, even when it gets hard.
- **Gentleness**—The fruit of gentleness is soft and kind, it does not lash out, and it is loving toward others.
- **Self-control**—This fruit is sometimes the hardest to show. Self-control is keeping your actions under control, even when you are very angry or tempted to sin.

Now look back over this list of fruits and see if you can think of an example of how you can show at least one of them this week.

**Dear Jesus, please help me show the fruit of .................. this week to others. Thank You for helping me show this fruit. Amen.**

Remember . . .

**God's Word is *for me* and *to me*, it is *in me* and working *through me*, and just like His love, it goes on and on forever!**

“Pray to me, and I will answer you. I will tell you important secrets.

You have never heard these things before.”

Jeremiah 33:3

Week 11

# Ring, Ring!

Do you know any phone numbers by heart? Can you say them? This week's verse, Jeremiah 33:3, is known as God's phone number. Even though God does not actually use a phone to talk with us, He wants us to call to Him anytime, and He promises to answer!

## Talking to God

Think about it this way. When you are talking to a friend, one of you is talking and the other is listening. That is the way communication works. Well, prayer is the talking part of our relationship with God. *He wants you to call Him*. And when you do, you get to tell Him anything and everything that is on your heart, knowing that He is listening.

## God's Answer

In this verse, God makes two promises. The first promise He makes is that when you pray to Him, He *will* answer you! Whether or not you feel like it, God is always listening when you talk to Him. He is never too far or too busy to answer your call. The second promise God makes in this verse is that when we pray to Him, He may very well answer in a way that we cannot even imagine! He wants to show us wonderful things, if only we will call on Him.

Many of us say our prayers before meals, at bedtime, or even at special events with our families. But is there ever a time when you pray, when you call on God, all by yourself? These can be very special times of prayer, just between you and Him. Will you try this tonight? After you are all tucked in, by yourself in your bed, call upon God. Say your verse for this week in your heart, and pray quietly to Him. Tell Him about your day, how you are feeling, and

anything else you are thinking about. Ask Him any questions you have, and don't forget to thank Him for all He has done for you. Then you will know what it is like to use God's phone number!

**Dear Father, I want to call upon You and talk to You. Thank You for listening to what I say and for always answering me when I call. Amen.**

Ready? Let's say it!

**God's Word is *for me* and *to me*, it is *in me* and working *through me*, and just like His love, it goes on and on forever!**

The only temptations that you have are the temptations that all people have. But you can trust God. He will not let you be tempted more than you can stand. But when you are tempted, God will also give you a way to escape that temptation. Then you will be able to stand it.

1 Corinthians 10:13

Week 12

# Temptations

Julia was over at her friend Audrey's house. They were playing a game when they smelled something delicious coming from the kitchen—warm brownies Audrey's mom had just taken out of the oven. Audrey knew her mom had told her that they could not have a brownie until after dinner, but she wanted one so badly! Julia noticed that Audrey's mom had left the kitchen, so she suggested they each sneak just one brownie . . . after all, Audrey's mom would never know! Audrey was being tempted in that moment to do something she knew was wrong. What was more important: getting to eat the brownie, or doing the right thing? What would you have done?

## A Wrong Desire

Being *tempted* means really wanting to do something you know is a sin. Maybe it is pushing or hitting someone when you are angry, looking at your friend's paper during a test, or telling a lie so you do not get into trouble.

## A Way Out

In our verse for this week, God not only teaches us that we are all tempted in many different ways but also gives us a promise. He says that when we are tempted to do something wrong, He will provide a way out for us. Sometimes when you are tempted the best way to make the right choice is to remove yourself from the situation. God says He will show us how to make a run for it. It's a little bit like a quarterback playing football. The defense is closing in on him and he thinks he is going to get sacked . . . until . . . he sees it! There's a little clear path where he can run through the players and make it to the end zone—a way of escape! That is what God provides for us when we are tempted. We just have to look for it.

What are your biggest temptations? Do you believe God will give you a way of escape? What do you think it will be?

**Dear Lord, You know I am sometimes tempted to .................. Thank You for Your promise to help me find a way out of that temptation. Please give me the self-control and courage to take it! In Jesus' name, amen.**

When you are tempted this week, recite this week's verse in your mind. And now say this:

**God's Word is *for me* and *to me*, it is *in me* and working *through me*, and just like His love, it goes on and on forever!**

God began doing a good work in you. And he will continue it until it is finished when Jesus Christ comes again. I am sure of that.

Philippians 1:6

Week 13

# From Start to Finish

Have you ever made something special for someone? Maybe it was a bracelet, or a picture you painted, or even something you baked. It's always fun to start on a project, but finishing it is the most important part. Nobody wants a bracelet that doesn't fasten, a half-painted picture, or cookies without any sugar in them! You have to finish what you start if you want it to turn out right.

## God Starts the Work

The verse you will memorize this week will teach you that God is the One who started His work in you. He is the One who reached out to you and called you into a friendship with Him. Before you chose to follow God, *He chose you!* And here we go again, with another promise from God: He promises to finish His work in you. He promises He will never let you go and He will always be there, showing you the way. What wonderful promises!

## God Finishes the Work

You probably don't remember when you were learning to walk. That was a long time ago! When babies are learning to walk, they want to hold on tight to their parent's finger. That might work for a minute, but if the baby stumbles or lets go of that finger, he will fall down. So the parent quickly learns to hold on tight to the baby's hand and not let go. Just like that, God is holding on to you. There may be times in your life when you want to let go of God's finger and go your own way. There may be times when you are not sure if He is still there. Philippians 1:6 promises that He is always holding your hand, never letting go. He will finish the work He started in you.

Dear Jesus, thank You for choosing me and starting Your work in my life. Thank You for Your promise to finish that work and never leave me. Please help me always remember that You are right there, holding my hand. In Your name, amen.

What do we say?

**God's Word is *for me* and *to me*, it is *in me* and working *through me*, and just like His love, it goes on and on forever!**

From that time Jesus began to preach, saying, "Change your hearts and lives, because the kingdom of heaven is coming soon."

Matthew 4:17

Week 14

# Wrong Way

Imagine yourself on a bike ride, trying to decide which way to go. You start off riding one way and turn the corner only to see two giant bulldogs with no leash growling at you. You quickly change your mind and think, *I will go the other way instead!* Matthew 4:17 will show us how we can turn around when we are headed in the wrong direction.

## Turning Around

This week we will meditate on a big word: *repentance*. To *repent* means to turn around, or to change your mind. If you are doing things that you know are wrong, Jesus says you need to repent. You need to turn around and go the other way. You need to change your mind. Part of repentance is telling God what you have done wrong. Does He already know? Of course He does! But He still wants you to say it.

## God Knows

Can you think of something you need to repent of in your life? Is there something you have done, or something you are doing, that you know you need to turn away from? You may think you are the only one who knows about it. But God knows. Look at this list and see if anything applies to you:

- being disrespectful to a parent
- not being kind to a sibling or friend
- telling lies
- disobeying
- stealing
- putting yourself first
- leaving others out

When you repent of your sins, Jesus is faithful to forgive you and make you clean again.

**Dear Lord, I repent of my sin. I am very sorry for .................. With Your help I am going to turn around and follow You. Thank You for forgiving me. In Jesus' name, amen.**

Write this on a piece of paper this week and keep it on your mirror:

**God's Word is *for me* and *to me*, it is *in me* and working *through me*, and just like His love, it goes on and on forever!**

The grass dies,
and the flowers
fall. But the word
of our God will
live forever.

Isaiah 40:8

Week 15

# A Book for All Time

Have you ever seen the way a vase full of beautiful roses can brighten up a room? Even though they look pretty and make the room look nice, they only last for a little while. Eventually those roses will dry up and die. The same goes for grass, plants—even our own bodies. These things are not meant to last forever. They are here for a little while and then they are gone. But in Isaiah 40:8, this week's memory verse, God tells us that His Word—the Bible—will never die. It was written thousands of years ago, and it will still be here for all of eternity.

## God's Everlasting Word

The Bible was written over a period of fourteen hundred years by at least forty different authors. Can you name some of those authors? Some of them were fishermen and some were kings. Some were shepherds, prophets, and teachers. But all of these books from all of these authors came together with one message—the good news that Jesus saves the world from sin. That message is carried on in many different languages in countries all over the world, simply because God's Word will last forever.

## The True Author

The Bible also describes itself as "God-breathed" (2 Timothy 3:16 NIV). That means that the Spirit of God breathed life into every verse on every page. This is why we often say that God's Word is "alive." So even though there are many authors, every word in the Bible is put there by God. You can be sure of that!

This week, find a flower that you like and ask someone to help you press it between the pages of a book. As time goes on, notice how different the flower

looks from when it was fresh and new. As it slowly dries, let it be a reminder that these kinds of things will pass away, but God's Word will stand forever.

**Dear Lord, thank You for giving us Your "God-breathed" Word! Thank You that it will never die, and I can know that it will last forever. Help me keep putting it into my heart and mind so it can live forever inside of me too. In Jesus' name, amen.**

Each time you look at your flower, say these words:

**God's Word is *for me* and *to me*, it is *in me* and working *through me*, and just like His love, it goes on and on forever!**

Whoever spends time with wise people will become wise. But whoever makes friends with fools will suffer.

Proverbs 13:20

## Week 16

# Choose Wisely

Today we are going to talk about friends. Some people have lots of friends, while others have only one. Some people have friends who are quiet and shy, while others have loud and adventurous friends. Who are your friends? What kinds of things do you like about your friends? What kinds of things do you not like about them? If you could create your own new best friend, what would that person be like?

## Wise Friends

This week's verse tells us how important it is to choose our friends carefully. When we surround ourselves with people who make good choices, we will probably make good choices too. Spending time with people who are wise—people who love God and act like it—is a very smart thing to do.

## Foolish Friends

First Corinthians 15:33 says that "bad friends will ruin good habits." Just as we want to surround ourselves with people we want to be like, we sometimes need to avoid being around those who encourage us to do things that are wrong. When we spend a lot of time with people who do not follow the ways of God, there is a good chance we will end up acting like they do.

## Being a Light

Even though you want to have friends who are wise, it's important to remember that God is not telling us to talk to and play with *only* those types of friends. Jesus says in Matthew 5:16, "Be a light for other people. Live so that they will see the good things you do. Live so that they will praise your Father in heaven." So there are certainly times when we need to be a light—to show others the love of Jesus.

Who are you around most often? Do you find yourself acting like that person? Can you think of some people in your life that you would like to be around more often? Why?

**Dear Lord, thank You for reminding me that I need to choose my friends wisely. Please help me remember this as I get older. Thank You for helping me make good choices. Amen.**

Take turns having everyone in your family say this:

**God's Word is *for me* and *to me*, it is *in me* and working *through me*, and just like His love, it goes on and on forever!**

Jesus cried.

John 11:35

Week 17

# Tears in a Bottle

When was the last time you cried? Do you remember what were you crying about? Sometimes when you are sad it helps if you have someone else to be sad with and to cry with. This week we will learn that someone is Jesus. You probably noticed that this week's verse will not be hard to memorize! Even though this verse has only two words, it tells us so much about the heart of Jesus.

## When Jesus Cried

Jesus was traveling when He heard the news that His good friend Lazarus was extremely sick. Lazarus and his sisters, Mary and Martha, lived in the town of Bethany and loved Jesus very much. When Jesus finally arrived in Bethany, He saw Mary and Martha crying and He was told that Lazarus had died. That is when Jesus cried. Do you think Jesus was crying because His friend Lazarus was dead? That is actually *not* why Jesus was crying. He knew that in one quick second He could raise Lazarus back to life (which He soon did)! No, it was not because Lazarus was dead, but because Mary's and Martha's hearts were hurting. They were crying and they were very sad that they had lost their brother. When Jesus saw how sad they were, it made Him cry.

## When We Cry

What does this tell us about Jesus? It tells us that He cares about our feelings. When we are feeling sad, it touches His heart and He can feel the same sadness we feel. Psalm 56:8 (NKJV) even says God keeps your tears in His bottle. Think about that! When you are feeling sad and crying, God holds your tears in a bottle because He loves you so much and wants you to know that He is near.

Is there someone you know who is very sad right now? Write them a letter telling them that you are

sad for them, and you are there if they need you. Tell them how Jesus is holding their tears in His bottle. And if you need to cry about something this week, remember who is crying with you and who is holding your tears in His bottle.

**Dear God, thank You for showing me today how much You love me. Thank You for holding my tears in Your bottle when I am sad about .................. Help me remember that You are always near. In Jesus' name, amen.**

Let's say it!

**God's Word is *for me* and *to me*, it is *in me* and working *through me*, and just like His love, it goes on and on forever!**

"I am the resurrection and the life. He who believes in me will have life even if he dies."

John 11:25

Week 18

# Do You Believe?

Who is your favorite superhero? If you could pick one superhero to be for a whole day, which one would you choose and why? It's fun to watch superheroes perform cool stunts, and it's even more fun to pretend to be one! Do you *believe* in superheroes? Do you believe that they are real, or do you just pretend that they are real? This week we will talk about a real, live superhero. A man who lived a real life and who has more power than you could ever dream of. A man you can *believe* in. Who is this man? Jesus.

## Life Forever

Our verse this week comes straight from the mouth of Jesus as He is talking to Martha, the sister of Lazarus, soon after Lazarus died. Do you remember this story? Here Jesus says that He is the resurrection and the life. This means in Jesus there is *life*—He has the power to defeat death and never die. Then He says that *whoever* believes in Him will never die! This doesn't mean that our earthly bodies won't grow old and die someday—but Jesus promises that just like He was resurrected, every person who loves and follows Him will someday be resurrected and live with Him in heaven forever.

## Believing in Jesus

Jesus then asks Martha a very important question: "Do you believe this?" And she answers yes! Have you ever told Jesus that you believe in Him, like Martha did? Have you ever told Him that you believe that He is the living God, that He is the Savior of the world? Can you tell Him that now?

Dear Father, I want You to know that I believe in You. I know my mom or dad, sister or brother, pastor or teacher may believe in You, but I want You to know that I believe in You! Thank You for being the resurrection and the life so that I can be with You forever. In Jesus' name, amen.

Let's hear it!

God's Word is *for me* and *to me*, it is *in me* and working *through me*, and just like His love, it goes on and on forever!

"My people, who are called by my name, will be sorry for what they have done. They will pray and obey me and stop their evil ways. If they do, I will hear them from heaven. I will forgive their sin, and I will heal their land."

2 Chronicles 7:14

Week 19

# A Recipe from God

Do you have a favorite recipe? How important do you think it is to follow that recipe just as it is written? It is pretty important! If you don't put in the right ingredients or if you put in the wrong amount, the end result will not give you what you want. In this week's verse, God gives us a recipe to follow in order for Him to hear us, forgive us, and heal us. If we want God's blessing, we have to follow His recipe, which has these ingredients:

1. **Humble yourself.**
   Being humble is the opposite of being prideful or thinking you are the greatest person ever. If you want to humble yourself, you have to remember that God is much, much bigger than you. You have to remember that you need Him for *everything*! You can't do anything without Him. This involves being sorry for what you have done that does not please God.

2. **Pray and obey.**

The next ingredients are prayer and obedience. You need to take time to talk to God. This includes asking Him for things, thanking Him for things, and sharing your heart with Him. Instead of just praying to get something from God, you should think about praying to get more of God. And then God says that we must obey Him. We must do what He tells us to do.

3. **Stop your evil ways.**

God says that once we humble ourselves by being sorry for what we have done, pray, and obey, we must turn away from the wrong things we are doing. We can't expect God to bless us if we are choosing over and over again to sin against Him. Certainly we are all going to mess up and

sin every day. But if there is something you are doing over and over again that you know is wrong, God says you must stop what you are doing and turn around.

Will you follow this recipe this week? Can you name all of the ingredients? Which one will be the hardest for you?

**Dear Lord, thank You for giving me this recipe. Help me to be humble, to pray and obey, and to turn away from my sin this week. Amen.**

And let's not forget:

**God's Word is *for me* and *to me*, it is *in me* and working *through me*, and just like His love, it goes on and on forever!**

I do not live anymore—it is Christ living in me. I still live in my body, but I live by faith in the Son of God. He loved me and gave himself to save me.

Galatians 2:20

Week 20

# Christ in Me

Imagine a king wearing a beautiful, giant crown sitting on a throne. That king is the one in charge. He calls the shots because he is the one on the throne. He makes the decisions for all of the people in his kingdom, and they trust him to do what is best for them.

## The Throne of Your Heart

Well, did you know that you also have a throne in your heart? It's not a real throne, but it's a place in your heart that has only enough space for one person. Before you know Jesus, you put yourself on that throne because you want to be in charge of your life. You mostly think about yourself, you do things to make yourself happy, and you don't care too much about the ways of God.

But after meeting Jesus, a wonderful thing happens: God changes your heart. He gives you a love for Him deep inside of you, and you actually *want* to do things that please and honor Him. The day you choose to follow Jesus, your old self is gone. You're no longer on the throne—Jesus is. Galatians says that your old self died with Jesus on the cross, and He turns you into a brand-new person. This new life is actually the life of Christ—Christ shares His life with you. It's *Christ living in you* that makes you into that new person! Think about that for a second. *Christ living in you!*

## Who Is on the Throne?

When you do only what you want to do, even when you know it is wrong, you are on the throne. When you don't pray and ask God what He thinks, you are on the throne. When this happens, you need to step

off the throne of your heart and let God sit there! But how? You can do that by remembering to pray, by doing what God's Word tells you to do, and by giving God total charge of your life.

**Dear Lord, I know that my old self is gone and now it is Christ living in me! Please help me keep You on the throne of my life by letting You stay in charge. In Jesus' name, amen.**

*Christ in you* . . . say it loud!

**God's Word is *for me* and *to me*, it is *in me* and working *through me*, and just like His love, it goes on and on forever!**

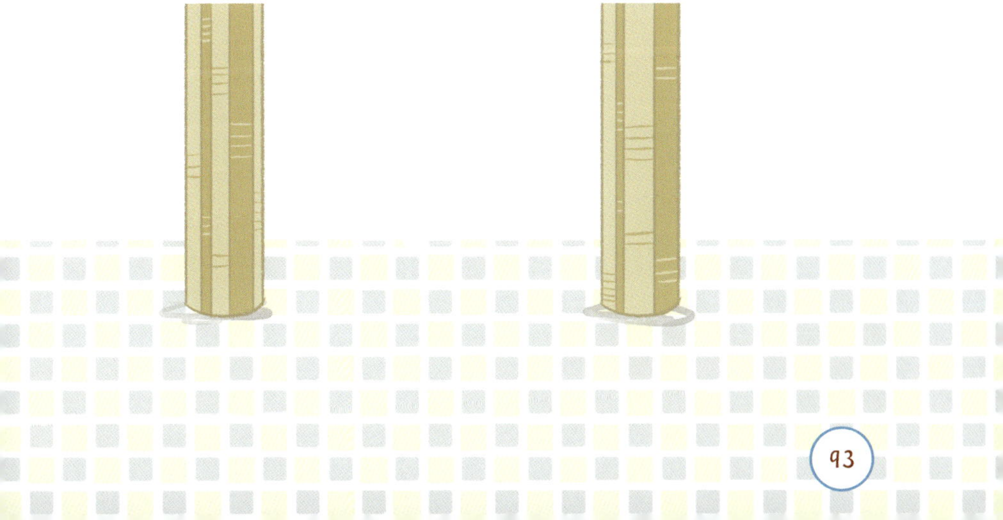

“Come and follow me. I will make you fishermen for men.”

Mark 1:17

Week 21

# Go Fish

One day Jesus walked by two fishermen named Simon and Andrew. They were throwing their nets into the water and hoping to catch some fish, like they did every day. Jesus called to them, telling them to follow Him so that He could make them "fishermen for men." Can you imagine catching a man with a fishing pole? What did Jesus mean?

## Why You Can Be a Fisherman

In this world, there are many people who have never heard about Jesus. There are also many people who have heard about Jesus but don't really know Him or follow Him. It could be they have never had anyone show them the love of Jesus. As someone who follows Jesus, you can be a "fisherman for men." That means you can look for people in your life who need to know Jesus more, and you can "catch" them for Him!

# How to Be a Fisherman

You are never too young to tell someone about Jesus. Sometimes it can seem scary, but after you do it once or twice, you will see how easy it is! There are two ways to share Jesus with others:

1. **Use your words.**
   Tell them there is a God in heaven who loves them. Tell them about when you first heard of Jesus and how He changed your life. Tell them what He did for them on the cross, and how He wants to know them and be a Friend to them. Tell them about a time when He was there for you.

2. **Show them by your actions.**
   Sometimes the best way for people to see Jesus is by watching your actions! Are you

loving others? Are you serving others? If your friends see the love of Christ in you, they will want to know Him and have His love inside of them too.

Can you think of one person you can share Jesus with this week? Talk with your family about who that person is and ways you can tell that person about the love of Christ—through words and actions. God will work through you to reach them!

**Dear Lord, please give me the courage to be a "fisherman for men." Please show me how to share Your love with .................. this week. Amen.**

Now, let's go fishing! And remember:

**God's Word is *for me* and *to me,* it is *in me* and working *through me,* and just like His love, it goes on and on forever!**

**If we confess our sins, he will forgive our sins. We can trust God. He does what is right. He will make us clean from all the wrongs we have done.**

**1 John 1:9**

Week 22

# How to Be Forgiven

This week's verse focuses on two things: *confession* and *forgiveness*. Let's talk about each of those words.

- ***Confession*** means telling God when we sin against Him. You might think it sounds silly to tell God that you sinned, since after all, He does know everything! But God wants to hear it from us—He wants to know that we are sorry for it. Confessing our sins is like agreeing with God. It is the opposite of trying to make excuses. It sounds like this: "God, I have sinned against You."
- ***Forgiveness*** is one of the greatest words in the Bible. To *forgive* means to send away. Because of what Jesus did on the cross, our sins are totally paid for—it is as if our sins never happened. So when God forgives us of our sins, it is like He sends our sins far away and gets rid of them forever.

In fact, here are four things God does with your sins:

1. He washes them so they are white, like snow (Isaiah 1:18).
2. He forgets all about them (Isaiah 43:25).
3. He removes them as far as the east is from the west (Psalm 103:12).
4. He throws them into the deepest part of the ocean (Micah 7:19).

But in order for Him to do those things, you have to confess. You have to tell God what you have done wrong.

Dear Lord, today I want to confess my sin to You. I know I sinned by .................. Thank You for Your forgiveness! In Jesus' name, amen.

After you confess your sins, remind yourself of this:

**God's Word is *for me* and *to me*, it is *in me* and working *through me*, and just like His love, it goes on and on forever!**

"Love the Lord your God. Love him with all your heart, all your soul, all your strength, and all your mind." Also, "You must love your neighbor as you love yourself."

Luke 10:27

Week 23

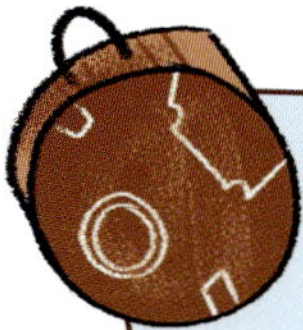

# Your Purpose

What is a *purpose*? It is the reason for which something was created. It is why it exists. Talk about the purpose for each of these things:

- pencil
- car
- chair
- piano
- hamburger

## Loving God

Did you know that you have a purpose? There is a reason you were created, a reason why you exist. In Luke 10:27 Jesus says what that reason is: you are to love God with everything that is in you. You are to love Him with all your heart, soul, strength, and mind. That means every single part of you! How can you do that? You do that by paying attention to what God says and putting His Word in your heart and mind. The more time you spend with God, the more you will love Him! You can also love God by making sure there are not other things in your heart and mind that you love more than Him. And of course, you love God by your actions—by serving Him and others. Always remember that before you loved God, He loved you first.

## Loving Others

Jesus says that once you begin to love the Lord with all your heart, soul, strength, and mind, you will learn that loving Him also means loving "your neighbor as you love yourself." What do you think that means? It means that you need to love and care about others as much as you love and care about yourself. For example, what if you were getting ready to eat your lunch when you realized your friend did not have a lunch? You could choose to eat your lunch and ignore your friend, or you could

choose to share your lunch with your friend or help her get her own lunch. Loving your neighbor as you love yourself often means caring about other people who are hurting or in need, even if you feel great and have everything you need. That is sometimes hard to do, but Jesus can help you!

**Dear Jesus, I want to love You with all my heart, all my soul, all my strength, and all my mind. Please help me love other people as I love myself. Thank You, Jesus. Amen.**

Take turns with your family, each saying one word of this sentence until the sentence is complete.

**God's Word is *for me* and *to me*, it is *in me* and working *through me*, and just like His love, it goes on and on forever!**

"I give you a new command: Love each other. You must love each other as I have loved you."

John 13:34

Week 24

# Dirty Feet and a Happy Heart

Let's start off with a game. See if you can find out what is wrong with the following statements: The rain is dry. The elephant is little. The snow is hot. The giraffe is short. Did you figure it out? That's right—it's Opposite Day! Try to think of some other things you could say if today were really Opposite Day.

## More Opposites

Did you know that sometimes the rules and ideas from God's kingdom are the opposite of the rules and ideas from the world we live in? For example, our world tells us that if we want to be important, we have to be first in line. If we want to be the best, we have to be in charge and think about ourselves first. But God says that if we want to be great in His kingdom, we have to become servants. We have to love others the way God loves us. We have to think about them before we think about ourselves.

## An Example from Jesus

Jesus showed us what this looked like when He washed His disciples' smelly, dirty feet. He was supposed to be their King, but He was on the floor washing their feet! Jesus wants us to love and serve others like He did. And when we do, He thinks it's the absolute greatest.

Have you ever done something for someone and felt very good inside? That happiness in your heart is God's blessing to you when you think of others first. He wants us to help other people and find ways to love them. How can you be a servant and think about others this week . . .

- at school?
- in your activities?
- at church?
- at home?

As you memorize your verse this week, remember to be looking for ways to love others. Have your family ask you one question at dinnertime every night this week: "Who did you serve today?" And have your story ready!

**Dear Lord, thank You for showing me how to be a servant. Please show me ways this week to love .................... In Jesus' name, amen.**

Say it!

**God's Word is *for me* and *to me*, it is *in me* and working *through me*, and just like His love, it goes on and on forever!**

**So if you eat, or if you drink, or if you do anything, do everything for the glory of God.**

**1 Corinthians 10:31**

Week 25

# Dancing Gloves

Do you have a pair of gloves? Take one of those gloves and set it on the ground next to you. Is it moving? Can it do anything special? Now, take that glove and slip it onto your hand. Shake your hand and wriggle your fingers around. Let your hand do a little dance. Now is the glove moving? Now can it do something special? Yes, it can . . . because it has something inside of it doing all the work! Did you know our lives are just like that? When we do something good, it is really because of Jesus inside of us, working through us. So when people want to tell you how great you are, remember to tell them who is doing all the work!

## All Day Long

During what times of day do you think about God? Many of us think about Him when we pray before our meals. We think about Him when we are worshipping at church and when we are hearing a Bible story. Did you know that you can think about God *all throughout* your day, not only at those special times? He is right there, by your side, walking next to you all day long.

## Giving God Glory

This week's verse tells us that *whatever* we are doing, we should do it for God! You might think, *You mean when I am eating my pancakes, I can eat them for God?* Sure! Because you are thinking about how He provides food for you, and you are bringing Him glory. To "bring God glory" means to make God famous. It means that you want everyone to know that He is God and He deserves all our praise. When you do something for God, you are bringing Him glory. And when He does something great through you (just like your hand in a glove),

telling others that He is the reason for your success brings Him glory too!

Can you think of some other ways you can bring God glory? What about when you are playing sports? How about when you are doing your homework? Can you bring God glory when you are running and playing? Think of some other ways.

**Dear Jesus, I want to bring You glory in everything I do. Help me remember that You are the One doing great things in me. In Your name, amen.**

Give glory to God as you say this:

**God's Word is *for me* and *to me*, it is *in me* and working *through me*, and just like His love, it goes on and on forever!**

"God does not see the same way people see. People look at the outside of a person, but the Lord looks at the heart."

1 Samuel 16:7

Week 26

# Looking Good

Sam is the coolest-looking kid around. He always wears the most expensive, most popular clothes, and his hair always looks perfect. A lot of kids are jealous of him. He is tall, athletic, and very handsome. However, Sam is also very unkind to others. He makes fun of his classmates all the time, says words he shouldn't say, and even steals from others. Truett, on the other hand, is far from being the coolest-looking kid. He is skinny and his hair is always sticking up. He wears clothes that are out of style and giant, thick glasses. But Truett is such a good friend. He is always doing things for others, and he is funny! He loves God and you can tell. If you had to choose one of these boys to have as a friend, who would you choose and why?

## Inside and Out

First Samuel 16:7 gives one of the most important lessons from God's Word. As you learn this week's verse, you will come to understand that who you are on the inside is far more important than what you look like on the outside. The world is full of people who can make you feel sad about the way you look. You might think things like, *I am too short*, *I am too skinny*, or *My hair is ugly*. When you think those kinds of thoughts, you start to believe them, and you start to feel bad about who God made you to be. But God says, "Stop feeling sad about the way I made you! Concentrate on who you are on the inside!"

## God Looks at the Heart

Who you are on the inside can also be called your *character*. What kind of person are you? Do you love others? Do you make the right choice, even when no one is watching? God says these are the things that make you into a beautiful, attractive person. People will look at your face, your hair, and your body, but God will look at your heart.

First Peter 3:3–4 says, "It is not fancy hair, gold jewelry, or fine clothes that should make you beautiful. No, your beauty should come from within you—the beauty of a gentle and quiet spirit. This beauty will never disappear, and it is worth very much to God." In other words, don't worry so much about what you wear and how you fix your hair. Instead, focus on the kind of person you want to be. That is something that will never fade away!

**Dear Father, I know You created me just as You want me to be. Please help me focus on my heart this week and the kind of person I want to be instead of what I look like. Thank You, Lord. Amen.**

Say this like you really believe it!

**God's Word is *for me* and *to me*, it is *in me* and working *through me*, and just like His love, it goes on and on forever!**

"Father, if it is what you want, then let me not have this cup of suffering. But do what you want, not what I want."

Luke 22:42

Week 27

# Finding Your Way

Have you ever walked through a real, live maze? If not, you may have worked on a maze printed on a piece of paper. The goal is to get from the starting line to the finish line . . . but the problem is that you can't see where you are going! If you make a wrong turn, you will run into a dead end, and then you will have to turn around to find your way out. Sometimes life is like a maze. But God has the perfect route for you to take; you just have to listen and see where He is leading you!

## A Very Sad Night

Jesus was in a garden praying the night before He was going to die. He was feeling very nervous and sad because He knew what was about to happen to Him. He would be beaten, made fun of, spit on, and worst of all, killed on a cross. But what made Him saddest was that He was going to have to take the punishment for all of the world's sin, just like it was His. He was perfect and He loved to please His Father, so this was very hard.

## Praying for What God Wants

Jesus showed us a super important thing as He prayed. He did not say, "Please, Father, don't make Me do this!" Instead He prayed, "If there is any other way to save My people, please get Me out of this. But if this is what You want, then okay, I'll do it." Jesus prayed that whatever God wanted to happen would happen. We should pray the same way. When we do, we recognize that what we want to happen may not be what God wants to happen, but we trust that what He wants is best.

As you memorize Luke 22:42 this week, pray the same prayer as Jesus. Tell God that when you are lost or confused in the maze of life, you want to go where He wants you to go. You might think going

one way is good, but God always knows the best way . . . and He will show it to you!

**Dear Lord, thank You for showing me how to pray for Your will for me. I want to go where You want me to go and do what You want me to do. Help me know which way to turn when I am confused. Thank You, Lord. Amen.**

Time to shout it!

**God's Word is *for me* and *to me*, it is *in me* and working *through me*, and just like His love, it goes on and on forever!**

Be kind and loving to each other. Forgive each other just as God forgave you in Christ.

Ephesians 4:32

## Week 28

# Giving Grace

Jackson was trying not to cry as he got out of the car to go into school. The day before, he had struck out three times in his baseball game, and his friend Cade had made fun of him in front of all his teammates. Jackson was embarrassed and feeling angry toward Cade. As he walked down the hall, he turned the corner only to find Cade trying to carry his lunch and books while walking on crutches. Jackson then heard that Cade had badly hurt his leg on a trampoline and had been in the hospital most of the night. As the teacher began class, she asked for someone to volunteer to carry Cade's books around for him all day. Jackson's heart began to pound. He remembered learning about the word *grace* in church. Even though he really did not want to, he knew God wanted him to raise his hand. He knew that it was the right thing to do. So he did. And all day, Jackson helped Cade get from class to class, carrying all of his things.

## What Is Grace?

Jackson showed grace to Cade that day. *Grace* means doing something kind for someone who does not deserve it. Grace means showing love toward someone who may have hurt you. Jesus is our very best example of grace. Jesus left heaven and came to earth to die for a bunch of people who sinned against Him and disobeyed Him all the time! When we deserved nothing, He came to give us everything.

## How Can You Show Grace?

Is there someone in your life who has hurt you? Could it be your brother or your sister, a friend or a cousin? Try to think of three ways you can show grace to the person who has hurt you, like Jackson showed grace to Cade.

Jesus says that we need to love even those people who do not love us. It is very hard to do, but

as you hide this verse in your heart and mind, God will help you!

**Dear Jesus, thank You for teaching me about grace. Show me who You want me to give grace to this week. Please especially help me show grace to . . . . . . . . . . . . . . . . . . Thank You for giving me grace when I did not deserve it! Amen.**

This week, write this on a piece of paper and put it next to your bed:

**God's Word is *for me* and *to me*, it is *in me* and working *through me*, and just like His love, it goes on and on forever!**

"I am the way. And I am the truth and the life. The only way to the Father is through me."

John 14:6

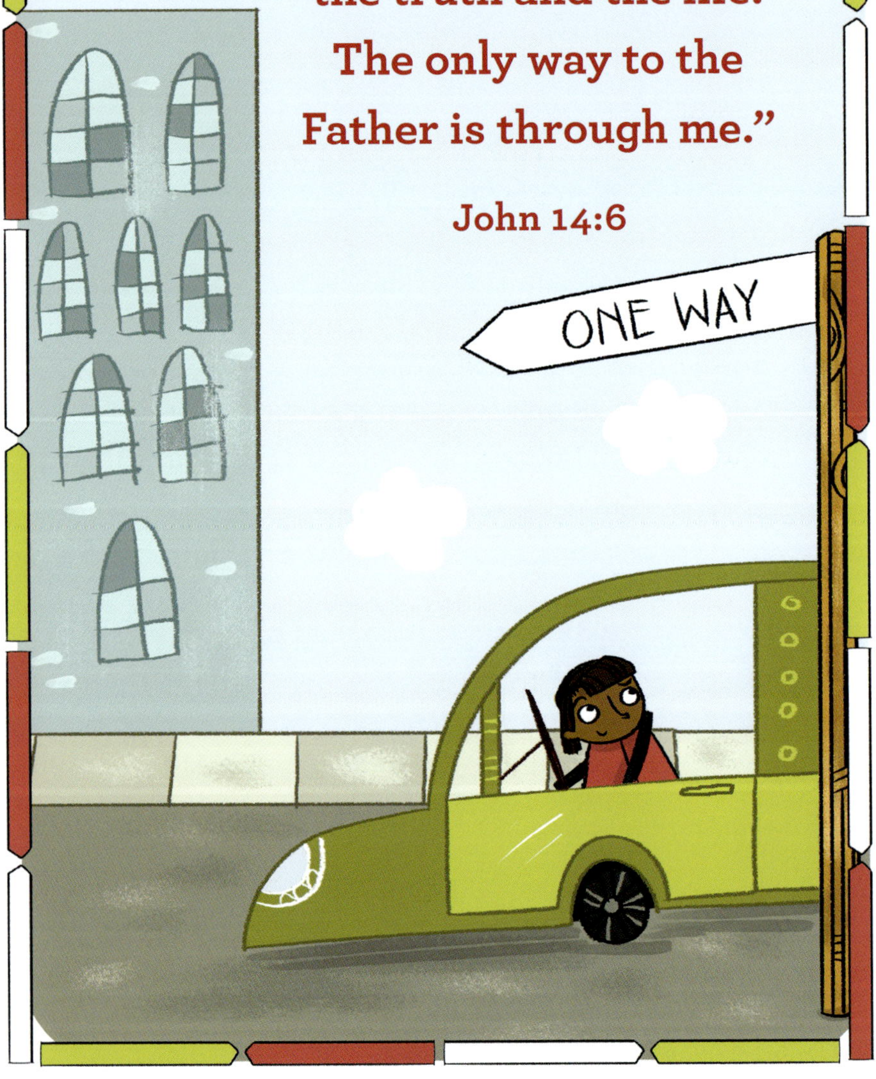

Week 29

# A One-Way Street

Next time you are in the car, look for a road sign that says One Way. It will usually be black and white with an arrow pointing the direction you should go. When you see a sign like that, it means that there is only one direction you can travel on that road. You can't turn left if the sign says to go right. And you can't turn around once you are headed down that road. This week's verse teaches us that there is only one way to get to God. Can you guess what it is? It's Jesus!

## Jesus Is the Way

The way you get to God is by believing in Jesus, accepting Him into your life, and knowing Him. It's by believing that He is God's Son and that He died for you. If you do that, you will be on the one-way street to heaven!

## Only One Road

Throughout your life you will hear people say many different things about how to get to God. They will tell you there are many different roads to heaven, and you can believe in anything you want and still go there. Some will say that if you are good enough and go to church, you can get to God. Some might even say it is wrong to believe that Jesus is the only way to heaven because it means all the other people who believe in different things (or nothing at all) won't be able to go. When you hear those things, think about John 14:6, which you will have hidden deep in your heart. Remember that the Bible—God's Holy Word—tells you that *Jesus is the only way*. In those moments, you can be sure that God will give you courage to share this verse and lead other people to Him!

**Dear Jesus, I know You are the only way to God. I will always remember that, and I will tell others too! In Your name, amen.**

You are putting a super important verse in your heart and mind this week, so learn it well! And don't forget:

> **God's Word is *for me* and *to me*, it is *in me* and working *through me*, and just like His love, it goes on and on forever!**

**I forget the things that are past. I try as hard as I can to reach the goal that is before me. I keep trying to reach the goal and get the prize. That prize is mine because God called me through Christ to the life above.**

Philippians 3:13–14

Week 30

# Don't Look Back

Think about the last time you were in a race. When you are racing, you want to go as fast as your body can take you, right? Can you think of some things to do to win a race? What about some things you should *not* do? One thing you should never do in a race is look back. You might wonder if the person behind you is getting closer, or you might want to know how many people are behind you. But if you look back, it will slow you down! You have to keep your eyes focused and your body pointed toward the finish line. Then you will go as fast as you are able to go. This week, Paul will tell us how we can win in the race of life.

## Looking Ahead

Paul was a missionary and traveled to many different places to tell people about Jesus. In Philippians 3:13–14 he was telling new Christians that they did not need to worry about things they had done wrong, or other bad things from the past. All they needed to do was look ahead to Jesus—and the prize of heaven waiting for them! When we are always thinking about the times we were sad and when things went wrong, we can't run the race that Jesus wants us to run today.

## Just Keep Running!

Is there anything that has happened to you that you think about a lot? Is there anything you need to put behind you so you can focus on today and tomorrow? Perhaps there is something you have been trying to do for a while, but you have not yet succeeded. Don't let that stop you—try again! Remember the prize you have in Jesus and just keep running!

**Dear Father, please help me stop focusing on .................. and set my mind and heart toward You and the prize You have waiting for me. Thank You, Lord! Amen.**

Share this with a friend this week!

**God's Word is *for me* and *to me*, it is *in me* and working *through me*, and just like His love, it goes on and on forever!**

You are young, but do not let anyone treat you as if you were not important. Be an example to show the believers how they should live. Show them with your words, with the way you live, with your love, with your faith, and with your pure life.

1 Timothy 4:12

Week 31

# Never Too Young

## Things You Can't Do

Sometimes when you are young, you can't do certain things that older kids can do. You may have been made fun of in the past for not being able to hit a home run or do a back handspring. And perhaps there have been times when you even felt like no one saw you or cared about what you thought. This week, you are going to hear some great news!

## Things You Can Do

First Timothy, the book of the Bible this week's verse comes from, is a letter from the apostle Paul to a younger missionary named Timothy. Paul is telling Timothy that he should not let other people get him down just because he is younger. You see, there is something you can do, even when you are young, to make a very big difference in the world! Read the second part of this verse, and see if you can find the five ways that you can set an example for others.

- **With your words**—You can set an example by the things you say. If your words are kind and you are encouraging other people, you are showing others how to live.
- **With the way you live**—You can set an example by the way you act. If you are making good choices and treating others the way Christ wants you to, you are showing others how to live.
- **With your love**—You can set an example by the way you love. If you are loving others, even those who don't seem to love you, you are showing others how to live.
- **With your faith**—You can set an example by having faith. If you believe in God and you know He is always there, people will see that and you will be showing them how to live.
- **With your pure life**—You can set an example by being holy and pure. If you are saying no to sins that tempt you and you are living the right way before God, you are showing others how to live.

Jesus thinks being an example to others in these ways is much better than being able to do big-kid things like hitting a home run or doing a back handspring. And guess what? Did you know that you can even be an example to your parents? Try it out this week!

**Dear Lord, thank You for showing me that I am not too young to be an example to other people. This week, help me be an example with my words and actions to .................. In Jesus' name, amen.**

Great job! Let's say it!

**God's Word is *for me* and *to me*, it is *in me* and working *through me*, and just like His love, it goes on and on forever!**

Children, obey your parents the way the Lord wants. This is the right thing to do.

Ephesians 6:1

Week 32

# Why Obey?

It was the day that all of Halle's dreams came true. She got home from school only to find a brand-new puppy. She named him Wilson and did not let him out of her sight for hours. When her mom asked her to take the puppy outside for a minute, Halle opened the front door. With no warning Wilson ran out the door and headed straight toward the street. Halle screamed, "Stop! No!" But Wilson kept running. You see, Wilson was not trained, and he did not know how to obey her commands. Fortunately, Halle was able to catch him before he made it to the street, but she learned an important lesson that day. She learned that there is a good reason why we learn to obey.

This week's verse is all about obedience, and it was written *for you*—just for children. It must be pretty important if God says it's just for you!

Why does God tell children to obey their parents? Here are three reasons:

1. Your parents have lived much longer than you have, and they know things that you

may not know. Like Halle knew that it was dangerous to run into the street, your parents know certain things. They are trying to keep you safe and show you how to live.

2. Throughout your life you will always have someone in charge of you. Learning to obey your parents is good practice. It teaches you how to listen and respect the people God puts in charge of you as you grow.

3. God commands you to obey! This is the best reason of all. In our verse for this week, God does not say, "Maybe you should obey your parents." He doesn't ask, "Do you want to obey your parents?" Instead, He says, "Children, obey your parents." That is a command from God.

As you learn your verse for this week, think about how you can do a better job of obeying. Practice doing what your parents say the very first time they ask, and see if they start to notice!

**Dear Father, please help me do a better job of obeying my parents the first time they ask me to do things. I know this is Your plan for me and I want to do it! In Jesus' name, amen.**

Here we go!

**God's Word is *for me* and *to me*, it is *in me* and working *through me*, and just like His love, it goes on and on forever!**

"Always remember what is written in the Book of the Teachings. Study it day and night. Then you will be sure to obey everything that is written there. If you do this, you will be wise and successful in everything."

Joshua 1:8

Week 33

# The Joshua Code

Hayes and Adam both loved soccer. They loved playing the game and wanted nothing more than to make the school team. Hayes decided that he was going to practice every day for two weeks before tryouts. But Adam decided that he didn't need to practice. He loved soccer, but he also loved riding his bike and playing video games after school. Which one of these boys do you think had a better chance of making the team? Why?

## What Is *Success*?

The verse you will learn this week will tell you how to have *success* in life. Do you know what that word means? It means getting something that you tried very hard to get. It means achieving a goal for which you worked hard. Hayes had success when he made the soccer team because he practiced for so long. If you want to do great things in your life and follow God's path, Joshua 1:8 will show you how. We can call it "The Joshua Code."

## Read, Speak, and Act

Joshua tells us that we should have God's Word—the Bible—in our minds and hearts at all times. We should read His Word, learn His Word, and speak His Word. When you learn your verses every week, you are doing just that! You are putting the Word of God in your heart and mind. Joshua also says that it's not enough only to read and speak the Word. We also have to obey it! We have to *act* on what we know is true.

Do you read God's Word in the morning? Do you read it at night? Do you think about it during the day? This week, as you learn this verse, remember what it takes to have success in your life.

**Dear Father, thank You for Your Word. Help me read, speak, and obey Your Word this week. Thank You, Lord. Amen.**

Can you say this without smiling while someone in your family tries to get you to smile?

**God's Word is *for me* and *to me,* it is *in me* and working *through me,* and just like His love, it goes on and on forever!**

“If a soldier forces you to go with him one mile, then go with him two miles.”

Matthew 5:41

Week 34

# Not One Mile, but Two

There is a saying: "Go the second mile." This week, you will learn what that means and why Jesus wants us to do it.

A long time ago, in the days of Jesus, Roman soldiers would travel many miles to different towns, most of which had been conquered by the Romans. As the soldiers were walking, they were allowed to ask a person of that town to carry their bag for them for one mile. They could not ask the person to go any farther than one mile. In this verse, Jesus is saying that after you go one mile and are allowed to stop, you should choose to keep going one more mile . . . a second mile! He is telling us not only to do what we are required to do but to do even more. When you choose to go the second mile, you are not doing it because you *have* to; you are doing it because you *want* to. And this is very pleasing to God!

Read these scenarios and think about how you could go the *second mile* (doing more than what you are asked to do) in each one:

1. Your classroom is a mess and your teacher is very busy getting ready for the end of the day. There is trash on the desks and books on the floor, and the chalkboard is messy. She looks at you and says, "Can you erase the board for me?"

2. You have a friend who had a very hard day. He got sick on his birthday, and he had to cancel his party. Your mom tells you to say a prayer for him.

3. You are selling lemonade outside when you see the elderly man across the street raking his leaves. He asks you for a drink.

Did you come up with some ways to go the second mile? Throughout the coming week, be watching for ways you can do more than what is asked of you.

**Dear Father, I want to go the second mile this week. Please show me ways I can do more than what I have to do. Thank You, Lord. Amen.**

And now say this!

**God's Word is *for me* and *to me*, it is *in me* and working *through me*, and just like His love, it goes on and on forever!**

I praise you because you made me in an amazing and wonderful way.

Psalm 139:14

Week 35

# Fingerprints

If you had to describe yourself with only three words, what would they be? Our verse this week is going to teach you three ways God describes you.

1. **You are different.**
   Take your pointer finger, shine a flashlight on it, and look very closely at the tip of your finger, on the side opposite of your fingernail. Do you see a design? Can you see some little tiny lines? Those are your fingerprints. No one on earth has a fingerprint just like yours. And do you know why? The reason is that God created you to be different from anyone else. Think of all of the people in the world and how creative God must be to make them all so different.

2. **You are special.**
   Yes, God made you different from anyone else, but He also made you very special. Are there ever times when you do not feel very special? Maybe one of your friends can sing better than you, or one of your brothers can beat you in basketball. Maybe you

don't like something about the way you look. Or maybe you wish there was something you were really good at doing. Well, God's Word makes it clear that even when you don't feel special, you are always special to God. He even knows how many hairs are on your head at this very minute! God has given you gifts—things you can do like no one else can. As you grow older, you will understand what those gifts are, and you will use them to honor Him.

**3. You are loved.**

The Bible tells us in Jeremiah 31:3 that God loves us with an everlasting love. That means it never ends! In fact, He loves you so much that He sent His only Son, Jesus, to earth to die on the cross so that you could be with Him in heaven one day. That is a lot of love! And do you want to know the very best part about God's love for you?

There is absolutely nothing you can do to make Him stop loving you.

Can you remember the three ways God describes you? Which one is your favorite? This week, each time you practice saying your verse, say this as well: "I am different. I am special. I am loved."

**Dear Lord, thank You for making me so special to You. Thank You for loving me the way You do. When I do not feel very special because of . . . . . . . . . . . . . . . . . . , help me know You are there and that You love me. Amen.**

You know what to do!

**God's Word is *for me* and *to me*, it is *in me* and working *through me*, and just like His love, it goes on and on forever!**

"The Holy Spirit will come to you. Then you will receive power. You will be my witnesses—in Jerusalem, in all of Judea, in Samaria, and in every part of the world."

Acts 1:8

Week 36

# The Final Play

The score was tied. There were only nine seconds left on the clock and Tyler's team had the ball. The coach called a time-out and brought the whole team into a huddle to call the final play. "This is it!" he said. Then he gave the play and told Tyler to make the final shot. He told Tyler he believed in him and knew he could do it.

Like this coach, Jesus called one final play before His time on earth ended. He gave His disciples one final instruction before He went up into heaven. Read the verse for this week out loud to see what it was!

Jesus is telling all of His followers—including you and me—that we will receive power from the Holy Spirit and that we are to be witnesses for Him, which means telling others about who He is. Let's answer some important questions about this verse.

1. **Who is it for?**
   It is for everyone who believes in God and chooses to follow Him.

**2. What does the Holy Spirit give us?**

He gives us extra power from God to be witnesses for Him. That power can give us courage to tell others about Him.

**3. When do we get the power?**

We have the power the moment the Holy Spirit comes into our lives—the moment we tell God we believe in Him and want Him to be in charge of our lives.

**4. Why do we need power?**

We need power so that we can be His witnesses. It is sometimes hard to tell others about Jesus, and we need extra help!

**5. Where do we go to tell people?**

Jesus wants us to share Him with those

around us: our neighbors, our friends, and our families. Then, if we get the chance, we can travel to other places, too, to be a witness for Jesus.

**Dear Jesus, thank You for the power You give me. Help me be a witness for You this week! Amen.**

Remember:

**God's Word is *for me* and *to me*, it is *in me* and working *through me*, and just like His love, it goes on and on forever!**

When someone sins, he earns what sin pays—death. But God gives us a free gift—life forever in Christ Jesus our Lord.

Romans 6:23

Week 37

# The Gift of Life

Can you think of a time when you received some bad news? What was it and how did you feel? Now think about a time when someone gave you good news. How did you feel then? Would you rather give someone bad news or good news, and why? This week, we will memorize a verse with both bad news and good news.

## The Bad News

The first part of this verse says that if someone sins, he earns death. When we sin, we deserve punishment, and that punishment is separation from God. The punishment for our sins is the opposite of spending forever in heaven with God. God is perfect and we are not. So the price for our sin is death. But wait . . .

## The Good News

Thank goodness for the rest of this verse! It says, "But God gives us a free gift—life forever." So yes, the payment of sin is death, but God has decided to give us a free gift of life forever with Him—even though we sin. Let's pretend you had a contest in your home: the person who can go all day without blinking gets a giant ice cream sundae for dinner. Now do you think anyone could win that? No! But sure enough, when you get to the dinner table that night, there is an ice cream sundae in your place! Your dad then explains that even though you did not earn this ice cream, he is going to give it to you as a gift. Why? Because he loves you. And that is

what Jesus did for us, by giving us eternal life when we did not deserve it. And that is most definitely the best news ever!

**Dear Lord, thank You for the good news You have given me! Thank You for giving me eternal life even though I did nothing to deserve it. I love You, Lord. Amen.**

And here is more good news:

**God's Word is *for me* and *to me*, it is *in me* and working *through me*, and just like His love, it goes on and on forever!**

**When I am afraid, I will trust you.**

**Psalm 56:3**

Week 38

# Big, Strong Hands

What three things are you afraid of most? Spend a few minutes talking about your biggest fears. Now, see if you can find a small ball. Look for a tennis ball, a baseball, a Ping-Pong ball, or a golf ball. Put it in the palm of one of your hands. Guess what? Just like you are holding that ball in your hands, God holds the *whole world* in His hands! The Bible tells us in Isaiah 40:12 that God has measured the ocean in the palm of His hand. It says that He used His hand to measure the sky, and He used scales to weigh the mountains and hills. Do you think a God that big and strong can protect you from anything that makes you scared?

## Give Your Fears to God

Trusting God can be hard when you are so afraid. But the longer you follow Jesus, the more you learn to trust Him. One thing that can help is to write down the things that scare you, each one on a small piece of paper. Fold up the papers, place them in a bowl, and imagine that bowl as the hands of Jesus. You are giving Him your fears and He is holding them for you! They are no longer yours.

## Remember His Promises

Another thing that will help you trust God is to keep reading and thinking about His promises in the Bible. When you memorize God's Word, you're hiding it in your heart so it is always with you. In those moments when you feel afraid, you can say Psalm 56:3 and remind yourself of how big your God is. This verse can also be your promise to God: "When I am afraid, I will trust in You." Just like God promises to take care of you, you can promise to trust Him.

**Dear God, You know everything about me, and You know all of my fears. When I am afraid of .................., please help me learn to trust You. Thank You for holding me in Your hands. Amen.**

You are doing such a good job putting God's Word inside of you! Say it!

**God's Word is *for me* and *to me*, it is *in me* and working *through me*, and just like His love, it goes on and on forever!**

Faith
that does
nothing
is dead!

James 2:26

Week 39

# Better Together

Graham crackers, chocolate, and marshmallows taste very good by themselves. But what happens when you put them together? You get s'mores! The individual ingredients are even better when you put them together! This week's verse talks about two different things that are very important in the Christian life and how they work together: faith and works. Let's talk about each one.

## Faith

Faith is a strong belief in God. It is being confident and sure that God is real and that He keeps His promises. It is very important that we have faith in our lives, because God is always looking at our hearts! If we do good things for God but we don't really have much faith, those things don't mean all that much.

## Works

Works are things you do for God to show Him that you love Him. You do good works when you follow God's rules and laws, and when you love others. If you have a lot of faith and you believe strongly in God but you don't care about doing good things, your faith may not be as strong as you think!

So you see, faith and works go together. It is important to have both. When you believe in God, you will want to show Him you love Him by your works. Faith and works are stronger together than they are apart! But there is one more thing to remember: God does not love us because of the works we do for Him. It's important to show Him our love through what we do and how we act, but He loves us just the same, no matter what we do.

Dear Jesus, thank You for giving me faith to believe in You. Please help me remember that I need that faith along with works to show You how much I love You. Thank You for loving and saving me no matter what I do for You. In Your name, amen.

Great job! It's time to say it loud!

**God's Word is *for me* and *to me*, it is *in me* and working *through me*, and just like His love, it goes on and on forever!**

Christ died for us while we were still sinners. In this way God shows his great love for us.

Romans 5:8

Week 40

# The Greatest Love

Imagine jumping with your friends on a trampoline. You tell them that you can do a backflip, but you don't want to show them. Do you think they would believe you? Probably not! Sometimes it is important not only to say something but also to *show others* that you mean what you say.

## Showing Love

The verse you will learn this week will remind you of how much God loves you and what He did to *show you* that love. Telling people you love them is a wonderful thing to do. But showing them that you love them can be even better! When you show people you love them, they know that it is true because they can see it. In the same way, we know that Christ loves us because He died for us.

## Higher Than the Heavens

Let's read another passage about God's love for you. Ephesians 3:18–19 says, "I pray that you and all God's holy people will have the power to understand the greatness of Christ's love. I pray that you can understand how wide and how long and how high and how deep that love is. Christ's love is greater than any person can ever know. But I pray that you will be able to know that love."

This means that God loves you more than you could ever imagine. No matter how hard you try, you can never understand how much God loves you! His love for you reaches higher than the heavens

and deeper than the ocean. And how did He show it to you? By dying on the cross for you. *And there is nothing you can do to make Him love you any less.*

**Say a prayer, thanking Him for His love for you.**

And now tell this to Jesus:

**God's Word is *for me* and *to me,* it is *in me* and working *through me,* and just like His love, it goes on and on forever!**

I have taken your words to heart so I would not sin against you.

Psalm 119:11

Week 41

# Hide-and-Seek

Play a game with your family: First, find a small object. While everyone closes their eyes, have one person hide the object somewhere in the room. Whoever finds the object first is the winner! Today we will talk about hiding the Word of God inside our hearts, where it will always stay.

## The Bible in Your Heart

Now this verse does not mean that you have an operation at the hospital and have a Bible put into your heart, right? That would be crazy. But by memorizing a verse each week, you are doing something incredible. You are hiding God's Word in your heart. You are taking His words to heart and knowing His Word *by* heart. The more you say something, the more you think it is true. And the more you think something is true, the more you feel it in your heart. So by learning the Word of God, you are actually putting it deep down into your heart, to guide you and comfort you all your life.

Let's talk about some reasons why we should hide God's Word in our hearts. Based on your verse for this week, what do you think?

- **So that we will not sin against God**—When you know God's Word and it is in you, you will remember the things He has said as you make choices throughout your life. Many times those words will keep you from doing something you should not do. The Holy Spirit will bring those words to your mind, and you will remember and obey.
- **So that it can always be with us**—Whenever you are away from home and don't have a Bible, you will always have God's Word in your heart and mind! You will be able to say the verses that God brings to your mind, and they will always be with you.

- **Because that is how God speaks to us**—There will be times in your life when you are scared, sad, or don't know what to do. In those moments, the Lord will bring these verses to your mind and He will speak to you through them. He will comfort you, encourage you, and remind you of His love.

**Dear Father, thank You for Your Word. Please help me hide it in my heart so it will always be there and help me not sin against You. Please speak to me through Your Word. In Jesus' name, amen.**

Hide this verse in your heart this week . . . you will be glad you did!

**God's Word is *for me* and *to me,* it is *in me* and working *through me,* and just like His love, it goes on and on forever!**

I can do all things through Christ because he gives me strength.

Philippians 4:13

Week 42

# Tired of Trying?

Imagine you a have a puppy in your house and someone left a bowl of dog food on your kitchen counter. Your puppy smells that food, and she tries to jump up onto the counter. She is not big enough to make it, and as hard as she tries, she is not even coming close. After trying many times on her own, the puppy runs over to you, whining, as if she is asking for your help. If she would have just done that in the first place, she would not have worn herself out! She could have stopped trying and come to you first.

## God's Strength

Sometimes you are just like that little puppy—there are things you *can't* do on your own. You need the strength of God to help you do them. Do you remember one of the things you receive when the Holy Spirit comes to live inside of you? Power. This week's verse promises you that when you need His power to strengthen you inside, He will give it to you. When you trust in Him, He will help you do things that are hard. You don't have to keep trying and trying to be good on your own. You can ask Jesus to do it through you.

## Our Weakness

Maybe you are nervous to talk in front of others and you have a big book report coming up. Or maybe you have to confess something you did wrong to a teacher or friend and you are dreading it. Is there something you are doing that you know is wrong, but you can't seem to stop? Perhaps there is something that makes you sad or scared and no one even knows about it. It could even be that you are trying

to get along with a sibling or friend. Just remember that when you can't do it on your own, you can turn to Christ for help!

**Say a prayer, asking God to help you with the one thing that is bothering you the most. Believe that He will, say your verse out loud, and watch Him do it!**

And here's a great reminder:

**God's Word is *for me* and *to me*, it is *in me* and working *through me*, and just like His love, it goes on and on forever!**

Even a child is known
by his behavior. His
actions show if he is
innocent and good.

Proverbs 20:11

Week 43

# What Is Your Reputation?

Pretend you want to draw a picture of a giant dinosaur. What might you need to draw it? You might find a picture of a dinosaur from a book or the Internet that you could use as an example, right? Just like that picture would be an example for you, you can be an example for others by what you do.

## The Example You Set

Our verse for the week says that every child has a reputation. People are always watching what you do, especially younger children. You are usually setting either a good example or a bad example. When someone says your name, what do people think? Maybe they say, "Oh, he is always lying," or "She is very kind." Whatever reputation you have, it is based on the way you act.

## What Is *Integrity*?

Let's talk about a word you may have heard before: *integrity*. Can you guess what that word means? Integrity is always being honest and living a life that is right. If you have integrity, you choose to do the right thing when you are tempted to sin. Integrity is making a good choice even when no one is watching. You won't always have your parents, teachers, or siblings watching everything you do. Sometimes you will be all alone and you will realize that if you sin, no one will know. What will you do then? It's important to make the decision in your heart before you get to that point so you will already know what to do.

How can you set an example for others around you this week? What will your reputation be?

I N T E G

Dear Father, I want to set an example of Your love to others. Please show me where I need more integrity in my life. When I am all alone and no one is watching, help me remember that You are there, and help me do the right thing. In Jesus' name, amen.

What? I can't hear you!

**God's Word is *for me* and *to me*, it is *in me* and working *through me*, and just like His love, it goes on and on forever!**

RITY

The Word became a man and lived among us. We saw his glory—the glory that belongs to the only Son of the Father. The Word was full of grace and truth.

John 1:14

## Week 44

# From Heaven to Earth

John 1:14 has four important phrases that will give us a lot to think about this week.

1. **The Word became a man.**
   So the Word of God—who *is* God—became flesh. The word *flesh* is the same as your body or your skin. It is the human covering to your soul. If God's Word became flesh, who do you think we are talking about? That's right—Jesus! He left heaven and wrapped Himself in a body to look and to live just like us. Do you remember why He did this?

2. **He lived among us.**
   Did you know that Jesus was actually on a throne in heaven, where everything was perfect? He chose to leave that perfect place and His perfect Father to come down to earth, where things are far from perfect. He was even born in a dirty, smelly stable where sickness and disease were possible, not in a clean hospital with fresh sheets like babies are today. He chose to leave His

throne and dwell among us. In other words, He chose to become one of us and live with us in our imperfect world, all so that He could save us from our sins.

3. **We saw His glory.**

   What is *glory*? The disciple John saw the glory of Jesus and said that "his face became bright like the sun. And his clothes became white as light" (Matthew 17:2). The glory of God is beautiful and breathtaking!

4. **He was full of grace and truth.**

   Jesus was a living example of grace. He was always showing us by His actions what it is like to give people good things they do not deserve. And He was full of truth, always pointing us to the Father.

Now you know more about how a perfect God in heaven left His throne to come down to earth. He was full of glory, grace, and truth, and He died on the cross for our sins. What a wonderful God!

This week's verse is a perfect verse to share with others around Christmastime. While you are celebrating Jesus' birth, remember John 1:14.

**Dear Jesus, thank You for coming down to earth to save me. I want to show You that I love You this week! Amen.**

And now . . .

**God's Word is *for me* and *to me*, it is *in me* and working *through me*, and just like His love, it goes on and on forever!**

"You must not have any other gods except me."

Exodus 20:3

Week 45

# No Idols

The verse we will memorize this week is one of God's Ten Commandments. In the days of Moses, people would build little gods made of gold and silver called *idols*, and then they would bow down and worship them. Today, some people still make and worship idols like that. But even people who don't actually build fake gods still make idols. Sometimes we turn things we love into idols—without even realizing it! Do you know how? We spend more time thinking about and doing things with our idols than we do thinking about and being with Jesus. Anything that you love more than God can be an idol, or another "god," in your life. Look at the list below, and when you see something that might be an idol in your life, put a little check by it.

- ☐ TV shows
- ☐ video games
- ☐ a toy or doll
- ☐ sports
- ☐ sweet treats
- ☐ clothes
- ☐ money
- ☐ music
- ☐ friends

If you can think of any more, add them to this list.

The things you checked in this list are not bad things. They all can be good things! But the truth is, none of these things can fill us up and satisfy us the way God can. God can speak to our hearts, rescue us, heal us, love us, and take care of us. Those are things that people or objects could never do.

This week as you memorize Exodus 20:3, see if you can do without something that is or could become like a god in your life. Give it to your parent or try to go one whole week without it. When you really want it and are feeling sad, say a prayer to God and ask Him to help you. Tell Him you are doing this for Him. When you do this, you will be showing God that He is the most important thing in your life, and He will bless you for it!

**Dear Father, You are the one true God. I am sorry when I love ................. more than I love You. Help me remember that nothing can compare to Your love for me. Amen.**

Say this in your favorite accent . . .

**God's Word is *for me* and *to me*, it is *in me* and working *through me*, and just like His love, it goes on and on forever!**

"Our Father in heaven, we pray that your name will always be kept holy."

Matthew 6:9

Week 46

# The Lord's Prayer

Do you pray? When do you pray? What do you usually say to God? This week, we will hear a lesson from Jesus on how we should pray.

The disciples spent all their time with Jesus, so they really got to know His habits. Many times they saw Jesus slip away into the mountains to pray. They even saw Him stay up *all night* praying! They knew that Jesus never did anything without talking to His Father about it first. So one day they asked Him to teach them how to pray. What He told His disciples that day, He tells us today too.

So how should we pray?

1. We should start by saying, "Our Father in heaven, we pray that Your name would always be kept holy." The word *holy* means set apart or different. The name of the Lord is not the same as other names. It should always be kept holy—treated as something special and set apart from everything else.

2. We should ask for "His kingdom to come." Here, we are praying for others who do not know God to come to Him.

3. We should pray for "His will to be done." This means we cannot come to God only wanting what we think is best. We have to tell Him that what He wants, we want.

4. We should ask Him for the things we need and confess our sins to Him.

5. We should pray that He will always protect us.

And that is how Jesus says we should pray! But remember, even if you do not mention all of these

things in your prayer, God still hears you. More than anything, He wants you to talk to Him. So do not be too worried about praying the "right" way. Just pray!

**Ask your mom or dad to read the Lord's Prayer to you out of Matthew 6. Then pray that prayer to God in your heart.**

And don't forget:

**God's Word is *for me* and *to me*, it is *in me* and working *through me*, and just like His love, it goes on and on forever!**

"The Lord your God is with you. The mighty One will save you. The Lord will be happy with you. You will rest in his love. He will sing and be joyful about you."

Zephaniah 3:17

Week 47

# God's Song

Have you ever been around a newborn baby? There are three things that newborn babies do quite often. Can you guess what they are? They sleep, they eat, and they cry! When a baby is crying, what does the mother usually do? If you were watching a baby cry, what would you do? When a baby is upset, the mother will usually pick him up and hold him close to her. She will rock him and tell him she loves him. She will sing to him and soothe him with her words.

## He Never Leaves You

Zephaniah 3:17 describes God's great love for His people, even when they had disobeyed God over and over again. He wanted them to return to His open arms so He could take care of them. Because you're God's child, you can turn to Him and rest in His love for you, no matter what happens.

## He Wants to Comfort You

When you know Jesus, He is always with you. *Always!* He knows just how you are feeling and everything you are thinking. And did you know that He is called "the God of all comfort" (2 Corinthians 1:3)? He will hold you and quiet your crying, like a mother does with her baby. Like that newborn baby, sometimes you might need to cry. Or there may be times when you are not shedding any tears, but you feel sad or confused, and you need someone to comfort you. God wants you to know that *He* is that Someone! Zephaniah even says that God will sing over His children. That is an amazing thought—the God of the universe, singing a song for *you*!

## He Is Joyful About You

This week's verse also says that He will "be joyful about you." That means when God thinks about you, He is glad! He loves how He created you and who He made you to be. He is happy about you and He rejoices over you.

**Say a prayer, thanking God for comforting you and singing over you. Then think of a song of praise that you want to sing to Him. Sing that song with your family, praising Him for the loving Father that He is.**

Say this very slow, then super fast:

**God's Word is *for me* and *to me*, it is *in me* and working *through me*, and just like His love, it goes on and on forever!**

"The thing you should want most is God's kingdom and doing what God wants. Then all these other things you need will be given to you."

Matthew 6:33

## Week 48

# A Key That Fits

Ask your mom or dad for their keys. They are most likely on a key chain, and they each look a little bit different. There is probably a key to your house and a key to your car, as well as keys to other places. If you try to unlock the front door of your house with the car key, what will happen? If your dad were to try the house key to get into his office, would he get in? No, because you have to put the correct key in the correct keyhole.

## Seeking Him

Just like these keys, God gives us keys to a happy life. Really, He does! He tells us about one of these keys in this week's verse. He says that if you want to have all of the things you need, and even some of the things you want, the key is to *seek Him first*. What do you think it means to seek God? It means to put Him first in everything you do. It means to remember to talk to Him, read His Word, and do what He wants you to do. He says making that your main goal is the key to having everything you need.

## Enjoying Him

God gives us another key to a happy life in Psalm 37:4. It says, "Enjoy serving the Lord. And he will give you what you want." What do you want more than anything? If those desires match the desires God has for you, He says that they are yours. But what is the key here? The key is to *enjoy serving the Lord*. This means to love God and enjoy God. It means to think about Him and allow Him to make your heart happy.

If you want to have a happy life with everything you need, what should you do? What will make you happiest? Eating your favorite dessert? Singing and dancing on stage? Being the star football player? You might enjoy those things for a little while, but

that happiness won't last forever. Those are the wrong keys. What are the right keys? Seeking God first and enjoying Him.

**Dear Lord, thank You for giving me the keys to a happy life. Please show me how to seek You first and to delight in You. I know those are the things that will make me happiest! Amen.**

Shout it out!

**God's Word is *for me* and *to me*, it is *in me* and working *through me*, and just like His love, it goes on and on forever!**

**I hope my words and thoughts please you. Lord, you are my Rock, the one who saves me.**

**Psalm 19:14**

## Week 49

# Too Late!

Madison was looking for her little brother Luke when their mom called them for dinner. She finally found him in the bathroom, and to her surprise, he had squeezed a whole tube of toothpaste into the sink! He looked up and said, "Quick! Help me put it back before Mom comes!" Do you think they were able to get all of that toothpaste back into the tube?

This week you will see how your words are like that toothpaste. Once they come out, you can't put them back into your mouth! It's just too late. That is why it is so important to be very careful with the words you use.

## Your Words

This verse is a prayer to God. The first part is about saying words that please Him, things He enjoys hearing. The Bible tells us that "careless words stab like a sword" (Proverbs 12:18). It also says, "If you talk a lot, you are sure to sin. If you are wise, you will keep quiet" (Proverbs 10:19).

## Your Thoughts

The next part of this prayer is about having thoughts that please God. Did you know that your words actually come from what is in your mind and heart? It is important to make sure that the things you think and feel are clean and right. In other words, if you are feeling angry or jealous toward someone, that may make you say things that are unkind. Both what you think and what you say should be pleasing to God.

## God the Rock

What do you think this verse means when it refers to God as a "rock"? Imagine a very large stone that is so heavy and solid that it cannot be moved. God is like that rock. He is strong and solid, and He will always be there. He is the one thing in your life that will never let you down—He will keep His every promise. All the more reason to please Him with your words and thoughts!

Make this verse your prayer every time as you recite it this week:

> **Dear Lord, let my words and thoughts please You! Amen.**

Keep it up!

**God's Word is *for me* and *to me*, it is *in me* and working *through me*, and just like His love, it goes on and on forever!**

Our homeland is in heaven,
and we are waiting for
our Savior, the Lord Jesus
Christ, to come from heaven.

Philippians 3:20

Week 50

# Heaven: A Wonderful Place

Let's talk about heaven! What do you know about heaven? This week, the verse you will put into your heart will always remind you that heaven is your home. Heaven is where we as Christians belong. We get to live on earth for a little while and learn how to love God while we're here, but then we get to go to the greatest place you could ever imagine.

Here are some things you might not know about heaven:

**1. Heaven is real.**

Heaven is a real place Jesus is getting ready for you. It is not just something we imagine or dream about. It is an actual place!

**2. Heaven is beautiful.**

God loves beauty! The Bible tells us that heaven has streets of gold, and the gold looks as pure and clear as glass. It has jewels in its city foundations, colors you have never seen, and beauty all around

(Revelation 21:18–21). There is no place on earth as beautiful as heaven.

**3. Heaven is a happy place.**

In heaven, there is no sickness! There is no death, no tears, no crying, no pain, and no good-byes. There is no separation, no sadness, and no sin. In heaven, we will be doing what will make us the happiest . . . worshipping God forever.

**4. In heaven, there will be rewards!**

Faithful people will receive certain crowns in heaven. You can receive a crown if you live a godly life, finish your life strongly by having faith, suffer for Jesus, lead other people to God, and teach His Word to others. But if you get a crown, you won't be walking around showing it off to everyone. You will actually lay it at the feet of Jesus!

See if you can tell which of these things *will* and *will not* exist in heaven: wheelchairs, crowns, mansions, ambulances, policemen.

God's Word also says that we will know one another in heaven. Do you know someone who has already gone to heaven? You can look forward to seeing that person again! Think of all the wonderful things that person is experiencing by being in heaven. What a wonderful place!

**Dear Lord, thank You for the gift of heaven! I can't wait to go there! Amen.**

Let each person in your family say this:

**God's Word is *for me* and *to me*, it is *in me* and working *through me*, and just like His love, it goes on and on forever!**

**Jesus is the One who says that these things are true. Now he says, "Yes, I am coming soon." Amen. Come, Lord Jesus!**

Revelation 22:20

Week 51

# Last Words

The last words you hear someone say are sometimes very important. When you are leaving for school, or to go on a trip, you might hear the people you love say last words that sound something like this: "I love you!" "Be careful!" "Don't forget to brush your teeth!" You should always pay attention to last words.

## Last Prayer and Last Promise

Do you remember memorizing the first verse in the Bible, Genesis 1:1? This week, you will memorize and meditate on a verse that is near the very end of the Bible. It contains two things: the last promise in the Bible and the last prayer in the Bible. Jesus says the last promise: "Yes, I am coming soon." And with all his heart, John says the last prayer: "Come, Lord Jesus!"

## Get Excited!

When you think about Jesus coming back to earth very soon, how do you feel? You might feel excited, scared, sad, happy, confused, or nervous. Sometimes it's hard to understand why grown-ups are so excited about Jesus coming back when it means we will not be living on earth anymore. But here are two reasons to be excited:

1. **We will get to see Jesus!**
   After you have lived for a little while, you get to know Jesus more and more. He is living in you and working in you, and He becomes your very best Friend. Sometimes it's hard when you can't see the person you love. Seeing Jesus' face for the first time will be very exciting! Close your eyes, and try to imagine what He might look like. One thing is for sure, you will know Him when you see Him, and His eyes will be full of love for you!

**2. We will get to go to heaven!**

Remember what we learned about heaven? It is a wonderful, beautiful place with no sickness, sadness, or death. It will be so exciting to be in heaven!

**Say a prayer telling Jesus how you feel about Him coming back to take us to heaven. Tell Him that you can't wait to see His face and the place He has prepared for you in heaven!**

And now say this with everything you've got!

**God's Word is *for me* and *to me*, it is *in me* and working *through me*, and just like His love, it goes on and on forever!**

Now, everything has been heard. Here is my final advice: Honor God and obey his commands.

Ecclesiastes 12:13

Week 52

# Wise Advice

You made it! As you work on your verse this week, think about how much of God's Word is now living inside of your heart. His Word will always be there and you will carry it with you forever. Never stop putting God's Word into your mind and heart!

Solomon, the wisest man who ever lived, wrote the book of Ecclesiastes. So if we know that every word in the Bible is actually put there by the Holy Spirit, and we know that Solomon was the smartest person ever, we better pay attention to this last verse! Solomon tells us that living this Christian life really comes down to two things. What are they?

1. **Honor God.**
   God deserves all the praise, devotion, and serious respect we could possibly give Him. To honor God means to remember that He is very big and very holy. He is the King of kings, and He holds the world in His hands. He can do anything and be anywhere. God is like no other. When you think about those things and feel amazed by them, you

are honoring Him. You are recognizing how awesome and great He is!

2. **Obey His commands.**

   God has given us instructions on how to live, and how to love and serve others. He has told us what He wants us to do and what He wants us to avoid doing. It is our job to keep those commands by obeying Him. Do we keep those commands because we want God to love us more? Do we keep them because we want to be sure we will get into heaven, or because our parents make us? No! These are not good reasons to keep God's commands. We should obey God because it is our way to show Him that we love Him.

**Dear Lord, I know the most important things I can do are honoring You and keeping Your commandments. Help me do those things as I hide this verse in my heart. Amen.**

One last time . . . louder than ever!

**God's Word is *for me* and *to me*, it is *in me* and working *through me*, and just like His love, it goes on and on forever!**

# Appendix

## Tips for Helping Your Child Memorize Scripture

1. Take one phrase at a time and repeat it over and over with your child. Once he has mastered that phrase, move on to the next one, building on each one until he can say the entire verse.

2. Put a dry-erase board in a high-traffic area of your home and write the verse of the week on it. This will serve as a reminder to you and your child to keep reviewing it. Have the board within view of your dining room table so you can talk about it during meals.

3. Use a dry-erase marker to write the verse on your child's mirror.

4. Write the verse on an index card and keep it in your car. Start the verse by saying the first word, then take turns with your child, each of you saying a word from the verse until you have said the whole verse.

5. Scramble the words of the verse on a piece of paper and have your child unscramble them, putting them in the correct order.

6. Put the words of the verse to a simple tune. Sing this tune each day and during bed-time routines.

7. Use small rewards when your child can recite the verse for you without any help.

8. Bounce a ball to your child saying one word of the verse and have her bounce it back, saying the next word, and so on.

9. Use sign language or make up motions to go with the words. Have your child sign with you.

10. Have an older child write the verse in a journal, maybe even using colored pencils and color-coding certain words.

11. Use websites or smartphone apps to assist your child in memorizing the verse.

12. Most importantly, discuss the verse with your child. Talk about how he can incorporate it into his daily activities, and have him brainstorm ways to apply it.